Walking the Earth

Life's Perspectives in Poetry

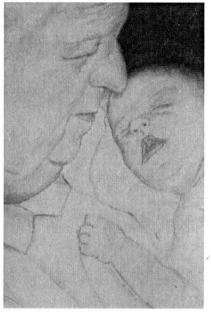

Editors: **Vivian Zabel**
Becky Simpson
Holly Jahangiri
Robert Blackwell

4RV Publishing
Edmond, Oklahoma

Walking the Earth

ISBN: 1-4116-4447-6

Dedicated to Vivian Zabel, better known as Mom to me.

Better Known

Becky L. Simpson

This is my Mom extraordinaire:
A dear teacher without compare,
Cross grammatical skill, a dare,
A child's love, her favorite fare.

She found me in a deep despair.
Taking my hand she said, "I care."
I could do nothing but pain share.
She did a mother's love declare.

Her smile, one of God's flowers.
Her laugh, one of His showers.
Her twinkling eye, another story,
In it is the Father's great glory.

My Mom, now and forevermore,
She is a part of my very core.
Unknown daughter not of her womb
But will be with her till the tomb.

Love you, Mom.

Walking the Earth

By Vivian Gilbert Zabel

Once we breathe first air,
We begin a journey
Along a narrow path.
At times smiles and laughter
Bubble through the sunshine
As we enjoy life's trail.
Yet, always, unknown, hide
Trials, tribulations, grief, and despair
In shadows along the way.
Sometimes we glimpse roses among
The thorns spread out by nature
While we hum love's lyrics and laments:
Desire, heartache, pain, and joy.
From childhood, young and free,
We too quickly wane to timeworn age
When traveling in faith to the end.

Table of Contents

Enjoying Sunshine

The fun, the funny, the lighter, brighter side
of life, even if a few clouds are included.

Chapter 1
Enjoying Sunshine

Awaiting the Thaw

Holly Jahangiri

Autumn-crisp leaves of orange, red, yellow
Whisper softly, "Winter's here . . ."
Around the corner, spring appears;
Insouciant buds play peek-a-boo.
Tiny blossoms poke, pink and purple,
Into springtime sunlight's warmth;
Night-time dreams of chilly autumn,
Ghostly branches sway in pale moonlight.

Then, riotous with scent and color
Hyacinth, iris, clover -
Eager honeybees buzz delight!

Taste spring's sweet bounty, dripping golden.
Heat waves shimmer on new-rolled blacktop -
Autumn calls from round the bend,
When summer's lightning thunders in.

Writing

Becky L. Simpson

A blur of fantasy and reality
Using words with natural frugality,
There creating some new abnormality
Or discovering a commonality.

Putting each sentence to a rigorous test,
Until eyes like blinking neon signs attest
An author we acknowledge has done her best;
This is creative writing at its finest.

Night's Gift

Vivian Gilbert Zabel

Night, with its treasure trove of stars,
Spreads its cloak of darkness over all below.
Like wings of a comforting angel waft
Hope through blissful slumber,
Midnight brings restoration through rest.

All we need do is gaze at the sky above,
Close our weary eyes, and let the sandman
Fly us through the sky to nestle
In the softness of eventide's arms.
Then sleep, my loved one, sleep.

Give Me Life

Vivian Gilbert Zabel

Give me life,
the real, vital thing
full of laughter, love, losses.
Imitation isn't for me.

Give me laughter,
even if tears threaten
now and then among the chuckles.
The joy outweighs all else.

Give me love,
even if pain and hurt
hide within my mind and soul.
The passion is worth the price.

Yes, even give me losses,
for though my heart breaks,
I know I feel, endure, respond.
Please, God, I simply want to live.

I Walk for Me

Diane Steele

The sun has not yet risen;
The air is fresh and brisk.
Each blade of grass is glistening
With an early dewdrop's kiss.

I sit on my front door step
And gaze upon the scene.
Morning has arrived again,
So quiet and serene.

I think of all the people
Still tucked away in bed,
But only for a moment
As I await what lies ahead,

This very special time of day,
The time I choose for me,
A time to put my spandex on
And very simply be.

To be is an expression
Of how I feel inside
As I begin my morning walk:
My senses come alive.

I listen to my Walkman;
I smell lilac-scented air
Not knowing what awaits me.
For this moment, I don't care.

I begin my carefree saunter
And choose my private pace.

It's not an obligation,
Yet, nor is it a race.

Stress free thoughts abound
As I slowly clear my mind,
And those I want forgotten
Are the tracks I leave behind.

The world becomes my oyster;
I walk within my shell.
The duration of this endorphin high,
Only time will tell.

But for this fleeting moment
Of my very busy day,
I find such true contentment
As I walk my cares away.

Learning to Read

T. Larkin

Condensation dilutes the ocean.
Speckled messages typed,
tapped out in layered letters
on this all-accepting
clean page.
Within the margins
hard-packed sand
takes the hand of the scribe,
absorbing the impact of every word
with dimpled simplicity.

Damn, I wish I could write like that.

The Brook

Robert E. Blackwell

The summer morning sun awakened
And cast delightful amber rays
Upon the quiet hidden brook
Beside my bed along the shore.

Within the water, dreams appeared
As sparkles playing blissfully
In quiet ripples gently floating
With the ever-moving current.

I sat along the water's edge
And watched those glittering sparkles
Until I felt the time was right
To enter the brook and grab them.

My waiting led to emptiness
When I found that those sparkling dreams
Did not stay where I expected
But floated with lost moment's tide.

The next day I awoke the sun,
And in its heavenward ascent
It shone again on the quiet brook
Where I reclined in contemplation.

My eyes beheld another dream,
Its sparkles dancing with the tide,
And I arose and took the plunge
Into the waters to meet it.

The sparkles did not break their stride
In passing me within the waves;
Having embraced the lesson learned,
I chased their opportunity.

What Now?

Jacque Graham

And God built
And created
And hoped for
And gave to,
And the world was.

And God said,
"The world must
Have light to guide
And warm it."

And from the warmth of His heart,
God created the sun
And presented it,
A token to the earth.

And from the softness of His love,
God created the moon
And presented it,
A token of Himself.

And from the gentleness of His mercy,
God created the stars
And caused them to light the dark sky,
A token of Heaven with all its promise.

And from the depths of His wisdom,
God created man
That we might light the dark paths
For our neighbors.

God still builds
And creates
And hopes for
And give to . . .
And we are

What Now?.

Song # 20

Robert E. Blackwell

I am refreshed
In the waves of dreams
That ebb and flow
In the ocean of my life,
Whose tides crest
Over the rock of reality
To wash it clean
And keep it pure,
So that it shines
In the noonday sun
With the golden sheen of hope
And confidence in its eventual
Fulfillment.

Anticipation

Vivian Gilbert Zabel

The boy, more than a child
But not yet in his teens,
Steps to the plate,
A bat on his shoulder,
To face the pitcher
Waiting on the mound.

A man waits, watching down
A long college corridor,
Looking for that someone
Who could be the woman
He's longed for years on end.
When would she come?

A bride stands inside the doors,
At the beginning of the aisle,
Facing the man at the other end
With love in his eyes for her.
Butterflies' wings beat time
With the music as she moves.

A young woman lies panting
While pains stab and tear.
Her husband's hand in hers
She squeezes in her distress.
He wraps his arm around her,
Giving what support he can.

The girl, for she's not much more,
Expects letters from the man
Who gently holds her heart.
His country's call took him
Far away from her and home,
To fighting, guns, and war.

The older couple sit side by side
In chairs at the airline gate.
Less than a full day's flight
And they would see their son
After apart for many years.
Would he be the same?

Challenges, pain, joy, tears
Appear at different times,
Creating heightened expectations,
Heartbeats' frantic tunes
Zinging bursts of energy,
Anticipation, anxious hope.

Notes to Ponder

T. Larkin

I find myself fascinated
by shapes of sounds,
and the curves
of your thoughtful silence.

Different chimes announce their form
in the music of the wind:
Some are deep and tubular,
while others sing with bell-like laughter,
but you, my dear,
you mold the notes around your being,
allowing each caress of air on skin
to define the melody.

The Rainbow

Diane Steele

They say beyond the rainbow
awaits a pot of gold.
I did walk the lucrative arc,
and if the truth be told

This spectrum of such beauty
can be found most anywhere.
When I reached my destination,
what wonders I saw there.

Unfolding like the pages
of a magical fairy tale,
the beauty of my lifetime
before me did unveil.

The pot of gold I realized,
an illusion, yet revealed
the value of the simple things
I often keep concealed:

The arc, the journey of my life;
the gold, all I've achieved,
the thought of those I cherish,
true perspective, now retrieved.

I turned around and gazed upon
the stretch that lay behind.
I knew that pot was only one
of many left to find.

Clouds Cover My Sky

Vivian Gilbert Zabel

Life's storms many times blacken my day,
While like a plant, I need light to grow,
And when angry clouds cover my sky,
My soul wants to shrivel and blow away.
Then I remember others too feel low
As their lives are battered and torn.
I reach within and search for strength,
Finding words that bring me warmth:
"Everything has its wonders,
Even darkness and silence,
And I learn, in whatever state I may be,
Therein to be content."
Give me the will to be content
Even when clouds cover my sky.

Path of Life

The journey provides perspective,
sometimes insight,
often just observations.

Chapter 2
Path of Life

Memories That Never Were

Robert E. Blackwell

I glance throughout an overcrowded house —
The sights are new to me, so are the sounds.
I'm sure it's mostly quiet as a mouse,
But not tonight; activity abounds.

The people within this house range in age
From very young to quite advanced in years,
And my gaze captures them in every stage:
Laughter, quiet moments, and falling tears.

Our heritage provides the common ground
I share with every person—him and her,
And thus my mind is cluttered with the sound
Of wistful memories that never were.

After decades in mystery's shadow,
It finally emerges in the light:
The branches of the tree, long and narrow —
A family out of mind, out of sight.

Even while embracing and shaking hands,
I am in mourning for what I have lost:
The chances gone beneath the swirling sands,
The bonds not made at a saddening cost.

It leaves me wondering what might have been,
And it throws my heart into quite a stir;
Yet, my thoughts are futile, chasing the wind
That bears my memories that never were.

The day passes quickly into the night,
And the time comes to return to our lives;
Separate paths that diverge with first light
To new wants and needs, desires and drives.

I leave behind pledges to stay in touch,
And take for my journey more of the same.
In reflection, I did not converse much,
And I struggled to recall every name.

I bring home a photo of smiling faces,
And with it, I allow my mind to blur
With visions of events, times, and places —
Consoled by memories that never were.

Alone

Becky L. Simpson

The sun sitting low,
Red sky harbinger,
Reflects six footprints
Leading to where I sit.
The sand, now moonlit,
Ghostly shows four prints,
Waves luminescent anger,
Yet peace resides below.

The moon races away,
Leaving blazing stars,
Their lights reflecting,
Like sparks in the sand.
Yet two prints withstand,
The stars begin winking,
Sky and horizon blurs,
No prints on display.

I sit, tired and alone,
My heart knows better,
There is one, I love.
Though far he seems,
My acts folly he deems,
from his seat high above,
For fears I must fetter,
If his love be known.

Defeat in Victory's Shoes

T. Larkin

Victory stands waiting for the start of the round.
Defeat is in the corner, staring him down.
Anticipation runs fingers through long, greasy hair.
Indifference checks the clock, and Time is aware.

Greed is making the odds and taking all bets.
Indecision picks Victory, who's never lost yet.
Fear and Loathing are now both feeling fine,
but with a couple of drinks, they'll get out of line.

Hope and Despair argue over who had the best chance
when Defeat and Victory finally get down and dance.
Surprise stands alone awaiting the bell;
is Success smiling there? You never can tell.

Discipline is with Honour, and they're both looking
good.
Grace sits with Decorum, but you knew that she would.
Impatience waits beside them, as if running a race.
Silence makes an entrance, and a hush falls in place.

The bell tolls; Victory swings, right up from the ground;
trips on a lace and stumbles, as Surprise laughs aloud.
Defeat lands one punch, and Victory hits the mat.
He was knocked-out cold, face down and flat.

Victory lost to Defeat for the first time in history,
and the reason for this is well kept by Mystery.
But Surprise and Mystery shared a knowing wink,
and I'm not saying nothin'... But it does make you think.

Exposed

Kimberly Ligameri

Yesterday I lived a lesson,
one I wished I never learned.
A man I believed in
betrayed my trust.

My tangled heart
is pierced with pain
from what I have learned.
His lies and deceit
trapped me in an evil game,
which I still pretend to ignore.
I was caught up in the chase
running after
false hopes of
a true friendship.

Yesterday I lived a lesson,
one I wished I never learned.
A man I believed in
betrayed my trust.

Through his deception
he created a man,
a man that did not exist.
He became a predator on the prowl
luring his prey,
studying his subject
carefully and close
until he knew me
like an open book.
He spoke in poetry
with captivating charm.
He focused on my needs
to secure my trust in him.

Yesterday I lived a lesson,
one I wished I never learned.
A man I believed in
betrayed my trust.

My heart is hardened
but has continuous fear,
containing the knowledge
he manipulated many lives.
I cry for those unfortunate women,
scorned by a
falsehood of friendship.

Unaware he is caught,
caught up in deceit
of his pathetic game,
his petty lies are shown.
He will no longer smile,
thinking he has someone's trust.
He will lurk in the darkness,
realizing he is alone,
realizing he is a shamed man.
May God take pity
on his dying soul.

Life is Good

Robert E. Blackwell

Today is pay day
And I jump out of bed,
Thanking the alley cats
Who give me my wake-up call
Every day around six AM.

Life is good.

I bathe in my bathroom,
Feeling the warmth of the sun
That balances the chill
Of the water I ran last night in my tub.
Good thing I filled it to the top
Before the Man shut me off.
With this bucket, I'm still good to go
For the weekend, and if I'm lucky,
I'll get it turned on again before Monday.

Life is good.

I primp in my bedroom,
Thinking about how smart I am
That I color-coded my clothes,
So that when they shut off my light
I could still get dressed in the dark;
Who needs artificial light for anything?
It's only good for seeing at night time,
And I go right to sleep when the sun goes down,
So I don't even need it then.

Life is good.

I walk sixteen blocks to work,
Just like I do on the days
When my money is gone
And there's none for the bus;
That's how I get my exercise,
Dancing in crosswalks with SUV's
Driven by cell phone slaves
Who treat pedestrians like Pac-Man® pellets
And oncoming traffic like the ghost monsters.

Life is good.

At work, my boss calls me in
To give me my check,
Which doesn't make sense
Because he never does that.
He hands me my pay,
Along with a letter
Thanking me for my services.
The job I've worked for fifteen years
Now has a new home in Paraguay,
And the boss and I weren't invited,
Which means only one thing:
I have a pay day Friday off from work!

Life is good.

It's ten AM now.
I decide to take early brunch
With all of my friends named Bill;
Their first names are Gas, Phone, Light,
Water, and several older ones
From a time when I thought plastic money
Was free money, and my only thought then was

Life is good.

By noon, my creditors are satisfied,
And I have enough money
To stretch out three dollars per day
For a week or more if I'm lucky.
Or, I can eat, drink, be merry for a weekend,
And celebrate my indefinite vacation.

Life is good.

Dream Castle

Vivian Gilbert Zabel

Gentle waves lap the shore,
Sending sea foam across bare toes.
As I walk along the sand,
I feel the only person in the land.
Sitting on the sun-warmed ground,
I let billions of grains
Trickle through my hands.
Then I scoop miniature dunes,
Pile and pat, smooth and mold
A grandiose castle, my Camelot.
Towers tall reach high above the walls
Where mighty knights should walk.
Dreams lie deep along the halls
That wind through the sandy keep,
Dreams which only live within.
Finally, I stand and gaze in awe
Of the masterpiece at my feet.
I turn to leave the peaceful place
Where I escaped my daily race.
Several feet from the sea,
I look back at my castle dream,
But the beach is empty, bleak.
The tide has swept it clean.

Cry Uncle

T. Larkin

Lovely, layered lies –
campfire tales in broken cadence
and memories of whispered I love you's
that cling hauntingly to the nape of my neck.

Now I count my fractured recollections,
brief reflections, dips, and deflections.
I count my own
rising inflection
in the inflection of a voice.

So there is no real choice;
there is just the passing of a brother,
an older uncle, someone's lover;
there is a passing of a father
amongst the passengers of time.

Yet another rhyme
has lived and died
on the memory echo –
and we all know
the river was made to drain to the sea.
And go figure,
fractured memories
make for fractured poetry.

Shadowbird

Holly Jahangiri

Rise, dark Phoenix, touch the sky
Let those who would lay claim
To each prized and precious feather
Try to soar on stolen wings

Their unearned flight as fleeting
As the wind that lifts, embraces you--
Casting them from their pretentious heights.

Even now, you would turn back
Risking gilded, earthbound cage
Borne down by conscience, knowing
It was you alone that gave them faith.

What silly creatures mortals are
To make your feathers into myths
Obliging you to save them from their folly.

Cursed, because you can, their need
A jesse, a lure—their loss
They never dared reach out and touch
The rapid-beating heart within.

A rush of wings, an anguished mortal cry
Abandoned by the gods of their creation
Maybe now they'll learn to stand...

Only then can they follow you in flight.

Sea of Despair

Robert E. Blackwell

The clouds of depression
Roil and ruin my serenity;
My heart is a charcoal cloud
That replaces my dreams
With sorrowful regrets.

My eyes are aflame,
Swollen with the rainfall of despair;
Tears overflow their banks
And spill in relentless streams
Of inconsolability,
Eroding the rock of hope
Into pebbles of helplessness.

I am cast adrift and abandoned to
Float upon the waves of my angst;
All I can do is to pray for deliverance
With either redemption or release.

A distant image begins to form
On the far shore;
It solidifies into a solitary being
Who stands watching and waiting
In a vigil as silent as my turmoil is not.

Her own eyes flow
With the rivers of sorrow
For pain solitary and shared,
And the clouds of her sky reflect mine.

Though she stands on the shores
Of her own strength,

She forsakes them and swims
Into my seas to meet me,
Joining her sorrows to mine.

Together, we become our own vessel;
We have no planned destination,
But we will travel side by side
Wherever our journey takes us.

Before the Day

Becky L. Simpson

My soul cried out, Lord, am I forgotten?
Your blessings, great Lord, fill my house.
Yet, there is something awry in my life,
But not material things I haven't gotten.
I search myself, sitting quietly as a mouse,
Praying, my soul in pain, pierced by a knife.

Tears escape my downcast blinded eyes,
Fleeing the tired face from whence they began.
My searching ends when finally it is known:
It is a simple thing, for which my soul cries.
God, I pray for a love these years to span.
My desire tugs as new cloth on old sewn.

It is my soul alone, which is lacking.
That which my heart most wants and desires
Perhaps, Father, him You have not made.
This is not a promise in which You're slacking,
For patience is needed to quench the fires,

And so I clasped my hands and prayed.

Fantasy or Life

Vivian Gilbert Zabel

So often you say you love me,
Yet you seemingly don't know
I cannot live in fantasy's fog,
Always in the blurred drug of dreams.
I need the clear, crisp light
Found in reality's realm of day,
Not the darkness of mere existence.

Come with me from still shadows
To brimming brightness of both
Dance and stroll, of walk and run,
The never dullness of movement,
Of song and lullaby, of tears and smiles.
Live real life just sprinkled
With dreams only occasionally.

So much lies beyond your grasp
If all you seek are wisps of cloud,
With nothing dared or hoped.
Step out from behind walls of doubt
And find me waiting expectantly
With arms wide outstretched,
As I welcome you to life abundant.

I Am Sorry

Robert E. Blackwell

I am sorry.
For the clouds of gray
I brought into your precious sky,
And more so for the rain that flows
Upon the landscape of your face
Each time that I misplaced the key
Of understanding you and me
Chasing your sunshine far away,

I am sorry.
For times I "thought," but didn't think,
And acted on such poisoned seeds;
For silence when a well-placed word
Could have turned sorrow into cheer;
For bridges burned and dreams destroyed,
Stumbling blocks that tripped your steps
And kept us from walking in harmony together,

I am sorry.
If I could turn back hands of Time,
Our lives would be sweet perfection;
But as the sands move through the glass,
I offer once again my love —
No doubt with imperfections,
But also a sincere heart and soul
With a helping hand
Attached to holding arms,
Enough kisses to create rainbows
Of smiles after the rain,
And rays of hope that I won't hurt you again.

But if ever I do, you'll always know that
I am sorry.

Lost Between

T. Larkin

My blood runs ripe with the struggles of the Serengeti,
and ancestral memory provides an escarpment view.

Or maybe not.

My soul ranges freely with the wild Norse men of old,
speaking the ancient tongue and drinking with the gods.

Yeah, all right.
No.

The words of kings and courtesans ring in . . .

Ahem . . .

I recall the mean streets of home.
Okay,
the sorta mean streets.
Yep, the clean streets of suburbia.
A white bred, white-bread boy.
A salmon-catching relaxinator, lotus-eating-son of lazy.
The grandson of a librarian/poet – whom I never knew,
on one side
and a machinist/labourer – whom I never knew,
on the other,
I sit uncomfortably somewhere between
viewing the schism – the chasm –
as a poor imitation of both.

Unlearned in either discipline,
I wear the masks that mark my fakery,
slipping from one the other without ever
finding a face of my own.

In Honor

Vivian Gilbert Zabel

The building wall rose at a right angle
Parallel to the sidewalk where I walked,
On each brick a name embossed,
A name of each one who served
Through World War Two.
I always stopped and let my eyes
Search the bricks for a special epithet,
A unique brick that to my child's mind
Glowed with extra valor and might.
"Raymond Gilbert - USAF," it read,
For the father I still adored.

A jet flies overhead toward
The Air Force base not many miles away.
I always stop and watch, imagining
The pilot, wondering if he's alone
Or if he has someone to guide him,
Sitting in the seat directly behind.
Somewhere a plane plays hide-and-seek,
Hopefully only with some clouds,
Where my son plots courses and rendezvous
Away from his wife and home,
All to keep us from enemy harm.

What owe we to men and women
From past to the present,
Who gave and give up even life itself
To take up arms and stand a barricade
Between us and loss of liberty?
How can we e'er repay the debt
To those who gave their all?
We owe more than we can give,
But the only thing they ever asked
Was we simply say, "Thank you."

*Dedicated to Major Robert Lee Zabel, Jr. and
T/Sgt. Raymond L. Gilbert*

Plastic Flower
Robert E. Blackwell

The vase on my table
Catches the gleam
Of the morning sun,
And when I tap the glass
Small ripples flow
Across the water's surface.

A large sunflower stands
In the midst of the vase,
Its bright golden petals
Crowning the cheerful mood
Upon its brown face.

I notice that for all its loneliness,
Having no friends nor family
And spending each day
In solitary vigil on my table,
Its cheerful mood remains
As bright as the sun outdoors.

My flower is made of plastic —
Its disposition given immortality
By acrylic paint and polymers,
Frozen in perpetual cheer
With which it both mocks me
And teaches me the lesson
Of suppressing and internalizing
All thoughts and feelings
Until nothing's left but the mask
Made of a smile.

It's My Life

Diane Steele

Tell me not to worry,
It's all a state-of-mind.
If that is the case,
Why is life unkind?

My thoughts are the essence
Of everything I do,
Yet in deep depression,
I haven't got a clue.

My life is a shambles,
But I know I can deceive.
The smile I flash outwards,
My heart does not believe

I know it is self-pity:
All I think about is me.
The answer lies within
While blind eyes will never see.

The child whom I hug each day,
A kiss upon my cheek,
Sits in total silence.
The thought does make me weak.

I rise above the darkness,
Break the silence with my voice.
I have to take a stand --
I know I have a choice.

I can wallow in self-pity
Or start to live my life,
Say hello to blessings,
And wave good-bye to strife.

Life's Trail

Vivian Gilbert Zabel

I stand nearly invisible
at the end of life's trail,
not many more miles
to travel before it's over,
but I never meant to fade.
Guess those of us who age
disappear to those still young.
To others who don't know,
I stand alone, while they
just wish the trip was through
and I would be gone from view.
But, listen, you who care not
for anyone but yourselves;
you don't know me.

Even if you don't expect
those who seem old to you
to have any use on earth,
there's so much more to understand
than the limited knowledge
that you ever possessed.
We give meaning to life itself.
We pave the way for all
who follow us along the path.
Our strength and endurance
have provided meaning and
hope and joy and power
to everyone around us.

Hear me well, world,
God has given me the core
within that gives me mettle,
but I am the reason that
I will stay alive,
continuing to be productive

in at least some small way,
until the end of the trail
no longer hides from me.

The Simple Things

Diane Steele

The simple things in life are those
that I enjoy the most:
a time to set inhibitions free,
and let my stressed mind coast.

I know we all have different ways
to chill, relax, unwind,
Yet our common goal, it seems,
is the happiness we find.

I know tonight I'll lie in bed
and pray that morning brings
what makes me feel so good inside,
the very simple things:

Feeling my son's gentle kiss,
hearing his young voice,
knowing in this lifetime
I am not without a choice,

Enjoying precious moments
Of every single day,
Making happy memories
to safely tuck away.

So I can sit and write about
All that life does bring
Is a treasure, cherished --
Such a simple thing

Open Mic

Robert E. Blackwell

As I gaze upon a small stage
That barely holds a singer
Whose fingers are glued to his guitar,
The question forms again in my mind:

What the heck am I doing here?

I feel as out-of-place
As a milk bucket under a bull,
Surrounded by young adults
And adult wannabes,
Crowded into a secluded café
That missed the bus to this century.

What the heck am I doing here?

In this darkened neighborhood café,
The "here and now" is "there and then,"
A living testament to the '60s,
Where the walls and the people are plastered
In the ancient rituals of anarchy.
Students, both actual and alleged,
Cloak tables and booths with ambivalence;
They partake of liquid destruction
Strong enough to power my car
From New York to L.A. several times over.

What the heck am I doing here?

The stage soon becomes empty,
Devoid of the singer and his pet rock......guitar;
I sip from a glass of hard apple cider

While pondering whether to take the stage
Or cling to the bar and join my friends du jour
On their ride to oblivion,
Wondering again from time to time:

What the heck am I doing here?

I take a step forward, and then take a few more
Until I walk out the door of the café,
Through a cloud of smoke that matched
The ones between the smokers' ears.
As I drove home, it occurred to me that
While I may have attended an "open mic,"
The patrons minds and hearts were closed
To every thought except for one
I'm sure they all shared with me:

What the heck am I doing here?

In Dreams

Holly Jahangiri

You're the one I long for when I'm dreaming;
Waking, sleeping, your smile I see beaming.
Every night and every day seems longer
As I struggle, all my fears to conquer.
When you are near me, you make me secure.
When you are far, each moment I endure
All alone, and full of trepidation.
Dreams sustain me through this separation.
I close my eyes, and you are close at hand;
Not far away, swept up in desert sand.
I'll sleep through every night and every day
To pass the time while you are far away.
I promise I'll find joy, I will not weep -
I'll hold you close when I am fast asleep.

Live Forever

Vivian Gilbert Zabel

Who wants to live forever?
So the pain of heart and limbs
Can endure ever lasting?
Discomfort will grow each day
Until I won't want to stay.

Talk of immortality,
I could greet my grandchildren's
Progeny for many years.
But when their time disappears,
I would be left just with tears.

I could watch history pass
With war, disease, desolation.
Leaders would rise and then fall,
Bringing hope, sometimes despair,
But never long-lasting care.

I don't want to live forever,
Not in this world we now know.
I want to know that some day
I will be able to escape
To a place not filled with hate.

Who wants to live forever?
In a place of cloudless skies,
Of love, peace, and endless joy,
Sunlight gleams without a storm,
Glory found in every form.

I will take forever life
In the place where He's alive.
To know that everyone there
Need not be separated

Nor ever feel incarcerated.

No pain, no illness, no tears
Will be seen much less known,
War, a word not even heard.
Yes, I will live forever
Once I cross Jordan's river.

Stop to Smell the Flowers

Diane Steele

Life sometimes does leave me
feeling lonely, stressed and sad.
I simply cannot bring myself
to say, "Things aren't that bad."

The time is quickly passing.
This fact I know too well.
As I watch my son grow quickly,
with pride my heart does swell.

Then life begins to brighten.
My resolve is but to pray
I find some simple pleasure
in every passing day.

For as the time is fleeting,
I'm wasting precious hours
trying to answer questions
best left to greater powers.

I free my mind of weary thoughts
of hate and wars and towers,
then simply take a needed break
to stop and smell the flowers.

My House

Robert E. Blackwell

In 1872, Susan B. Anthony was arrested in Rochester, New York for voting; women did not have the right to vote at the time.

A lonely figure stood
In a small six-by-six room
With doors of wrought iron
And windows likewise adorned.

The peace of her countenance
Contrasted with the uncertainty
Of the life she faced inside her cell
As a guest of her government.

Another figure watched her
While shuffling papers on his desk,
Boredom betraying the official bearing
That he tried to keep up with angry glares.

"You shouldn't be here."
The policeman spoke in soft tones
That expressed feeling inconvenienced
By her involuntary company.

Her silence annoyed him;
He became a tower of indignation,
Pointing an angry finger and
Shaking the walls with his voice.

"You should be at home
Taking care of your family
Instead of meddling in men's affairs.
A woman's place is in her house!"

The woman's serenity
Remained unshaken by the bluster
Of her reluctant captor's lecture,
And she spoke with quiet determination:

"Not just my House, but soon my Senate —
Today, a governess, tomorrow, a governor,
And some day, my place will evolve
From my house to the White House."

On August 18, 1920, Tennessee became the 36th state to ratify the 19th Amendment to the U.S. Constitution, which guaranteed women the right to vote.

Anthem's Refrain

Vivian Gilbert Zabel

Brilliant flares of light
flash across the velvet night.
The sky reflects freedom's glow.
Once upon a time
another watched rockets' glare
and wrote an anthem's refrain.

Hidden in the Shadows

Life has sorrows, grief, pain, and despair –
which we must conquer.

Chapter 3
Hidden in the Shadows

False Promises

Kimberly Ligameri

Tantalizing me with false promises,
you play me for a fool.
What a wicked game
I let you play,
believing in the bed of lies
you carry around so boldly.
I am the giver.
You are the taker.
I am the slave,
and you are the master.
You call,
and I run.
You ignore,
and I cry.
You speak,
and I listen.
What a wicked game
I have found myself in,
trusting you to be faithful,
yet you betray me again.
I can only blame myself
for letting you destroy my heart.
Deep down inside I knew all along
you were deceiving me.
Promises made;
Promises broken.
Living with these false promises
has only blinded me from seeing
you pretended to love and honor me.
What a wicked game
you have won.

In Memory

Vivian Gilbert Zabel

A flutter of life is swiftly felt,
Then more pressing is the moving
Until 'tis almost a constant thing,
This tumult beneath my breast.

A time of waiting, of wonder, of want
That slower and longer seems to grow.
Each time seems newer than before,
Although birth has happened times untold.

At last the days of waiting are over.
The time of work and pain is here
That soon will be but a dim memory
In the love I already feel.

A cry, a smile, a heart full of yearning
To hold this small thing of ours,
Then news so sad, so uncomprehending
Leaves arms aching with empty longing.

A small white box in satin wrapped
Is brought beside my bed at last.
It cannot be - she is only sleeping!
Yet her sleep is that which shall not pass.

In memory of Regina Louise 12-19-68 till 12-20-68

Cancer

Jacque Graham

The day is cold.
My spirit also chills.
Waiting for the surgeon's call
Dampens my mood.

"A port" they call the device
Implanted in the chest,
Designed to feed the body poisons,
Chemicals to kill the cancer
Fed by a cigarette,
Bit by bit,
Month by month,
Year by year.

They tried to warn us then,
But advertisements won.
"Be popular, follow the crowd.
Be one of the group.
Be attractive; buy my brand!"
They said.
What a lie!
Popularity bought at the price of life.

Cancer is a high price to pay,
Following the crowd of victims
Balding from the treatments,
The treatment that buys a little time,
But doesn't buy life.
Bald does not seem attractive now . . .
Too high a price for
Being "branded" by the promise of popularity.

Little Strange Girl

Kimberly Ligameri

She was just a little girl trying to belong,
curious about the differences between right and wrong.
An innocence surrounding, that made her seem pure,
letting others forget the terrible deeds done before.

She was twisted in such a way no one seemed to accept,
however they were suspicious of all the secrets she kept.
They frowned upon her promiscuous way.
They ridiculed her for running astray.

Poor little strange girl, crying in sadness,
what was it that drove her to all this madness?
Longing for her parents to care,
could that be what brought on all this despair?

Selling her body to feed her addictions,
never having any restrictions.
Poor little strange girl, look into her pale blue eyes,
there is such an appalling history that lies.

She needs to be loved and protected.
She is weary of being loathed and rejected.
The sun never shines on her withdrawn face.
She made her home wandering from place to place.

Many years she has felt invisible and alone.
Her confusion and sadness has only grown.
Poor little strange girl, can you hear her plea?
"Please God, let someone love me."

Dry Season

T. Larkin

Even a broken pencil can render an incomplete drawing,
and I —a broken-pencil poet— can strive to describe
another fractured moment
in a splinter of a life.

The topiary goat nods in agreement.
Someone trimmed his horns too much,
and now he looks a little less Billy,
but the frogs hide their smiles
while squatting on leafy haunches.

The mimes don't like it when I throw popcorn through
the invisible box;
hungry pigeons don't respect their act
as they swarm towards the free food.

The frogs nearly laugh aloud,
deciding instead
on a branch-by-branch round of applause.

The wind sounds like the whisper of a friend,
or is that the voice of the devil riding my shoulder?
It gets harder to distinguish the dragons from the tree-
line
after the sun goes down,
and the wind whispers tells me
that green survives winter
easier than drought.

I Cried Today

Vivian Gilbert Zabel

I cried today, tears of pain and sorrow
For the teenager who can't find her way,
For the elderly who need help each day,
For the grandchildren who have gone astray,
And for the ones who left but had no say.

I cried today, tears of anger and mistrust
For the politician who plays a game,
For the old one who no longer knows his name,
For immorality that seems to stay the same,
For the loved one who grows more lame.

I cried today, tears of grief and remorse
For the grandson whose birthday we can't share,
For the pain when he thinks we no longer care,
For the hole in my heart that remains so bare,
For the loss of him and his sister that I wear.

I cried today, tears of fear and prayer
For the ill among us that life is leaving,
For those who will be left behind grieving,
For everyone whose happy faces are deceiving,
For those who pray, hope, and keep believing.

Written on Faris' thirteenth birthday, Aug. 8, 2003.
I love you, Faris, wherever you are.

Nightmare

Robert E. Blackwell

I lie in bed,
Seeking the embrace of sleep,
But my fickle mistress fills me
With visions that frighten
And leave me streaming.

Thoughts of a future without you
Is a bitter gale
That snatches away the goblet of my heart
And sends it beyond my grasp
Toward the rocks of depression,
Where it smashes into infinite shards
Which scatter among the four winds,
Becoming dust in the very air.

The bile rises into my throat
And I awaken in a panic,
Desiring to retch and spew the nightmare
Bubbling up from my soul,
But it quickly soothes and dissipates
Into my belly
While I sit and contemplate
The terror of the moment.

I peer into my cupboard
And find my goblet there;
Though not quite whole,
Its shards are held together
By the many tears that fill it;
Even though it leaks it remains together
'Til the next night the mare must roam.

The poem is dedicated to all who suffer the indignity of depression. It draws an analogy between depression and hell. In my mind, hell is absolute hopelessness and fits so well into depression's mold.

Depression

Becky L. Simpson

Gnashing, rotting teeth, gnawing all hope,
Gaping, dark mouth swallows my strength.
Odorous heat brings red blush to my face;
Words become stinging whips in this place.
No measure may be made of its length,
For time is lost on this slimy slope.

Worms of doubt now inhabit my mind,
Leaving in passing decomposed light.
Whispers come to my ear, bringing fear,
Losing my grasp on sanity so dear.
My only thought becomes my swift flight,
Running, even though I am quite blind.

In this hell there is but selfishness,
Sullenly stealing God's greatest gift.
All grace hidden from my dim sight,
Unable to lead me home by its light,
I am left like chaff that the winds sift,
Until love's hand offers forgiveness.

Gently taking away all shame.

It Was Never the Big Things

Holly Jahangiri

Zigzag flash of lightning,
howling wind, stinging lash
of the deluvian whip -

It was never the big things.

Gnawing cancer, crack of brittle bone
Sharp stab of pain between the shoulder blades -
so real I knew I was alive.

It was never the big things.

You stole a beating chunk of my heart,
still slick with life-blood -
Snatched it! Took it to the grave, and left me.

But it was never the big things.

Partly cloudy, endless gray, no contour
to the rainless, unrelenting clouds.
I watch the dust motes settle. Swipe!
They settle again. The world looks muted,
strange - through a thin plastic lens.
A clock ticks.
Seconds.
Silent breaths...
and one
last
sigh.

I Never Said Goodbye

Vivian Gilbert Zabel

The call came unexpectedly, anticipated
since Jean had fought cancer for so long.
She battled the invader once and won,
sending him running for his life.
With stealth he returned in hiding,
waiting to catch her unaware.
The sides were drawn once more.
The doctors, with their skill,
her faith, her strength on one side;
he, with the Grim Reaper, grinning
with dark delight on the other.
The war waged long and hard.
Jean and the doctors won skirmishes,
one after the other; but each left
her body weaker than before.
Her will, her desire to endure,
faltered not, shining strong
even the last time we talked.
She asked me not to see her
lying weak and wan in a hospital bed;
she said, each time I asked,
to wait, she would be better soon.
I tarried, my heart sad and knowing,
but for her sake I didn't go.
I prayed for her healing,
but I never went to hold her hand.
I never said goodbye.

~dedicated to Jean Gilliland, July 21, 2003~

Once a Hero

T. Larkin

Time it is,
yes, for the borrowing of
a moment divided.
A fractured scrap of infinite length
lends itself to the binding,
leaving enough to blind the eyes
of the unseeing monument...
as if for execution.

The statue knows naught of its placement,
standing not where the sculptor decided
or where it grew from the natural stone,
but instead facing the sea
from an eroding cliff
not its choice.

Busy hands chose the station,
unknowing or uncaring
of the hidden danger,
resigning their memorial
to the ravages of weather
and the whimsy of the local shorebirds.

In the meantime the tide works the shoreline,
scouring the foot of the mountain
in conjunction with the wind and the rain,
leaving the statue to mutely express
its own demise.

Missing My Mother

Kimberly Ligameri

I have cried
a thousand tears
just remembering you.
I have felt the wind
pulse through my body
as if you were breathing into my soul.
I have closed my eyes
to hear your sweet voice
calling my name,
only to open them
and see nothing there.
How I miss
the times we shared,
you my one and only true friend.
I know I could have told you anything,
and you would have loved me just the same.
I have prayed
that you are in heaven now,
watching over me.
I have dreamed of the day
we will meet again.
I have thought of us
dancing and singing together
like we once did. How I miss
holding you in my arms, Mother,
you my one and only true friend.
I would have given anything
to take your pain away, dry your tears,
and make you healthy again.
Somehow that was last
in your mind, everyone else came first.
Mother, I miss seeing you.
Mother, I miss hearing you.
Mother, I miss taking care of you.
Mother, I miss all of you,
but most of all
I just miss loving you.

Views of Roses and Thorns

Nature provides flowers and thickets, roses and thorns

Chapter 4
Views of Roses and Thorns

Autumn Playground

T. Larkin

I love to watch the wind entice the trees to play.
Like in a child's game of tag, it touches each in turn,
running in short bursts from one to another.

The rustle of dry leaves reminds me of laughter
as branches stretch for nearby neighbours
and wave frantically at friends
just out of reach.

Slanting sunshine, and shadows from clouds,
dart in and out, racing ahead of the wind
to engage in a different game
with colour and light.

Bright red faces shine in the autumn foliage;
frenetic and out of breath they play,
as they cling to the last vestiges of summer.

On the ground the wind toys with the fallen,
rearranging the living artwork with playful palette;
using swoops and swirls to spread
a pastel drawing
across the playground.

Autumn Memories

Diane Steele

Showers of a special kind
Blanket all I see.
The colors of the leaf-drops
Bring memories to me.

I recall when I was young,
Leaves shuffled 'neath my feet.
The scent of fresh pine filled air-
A perfume, oh so sweet.

If I could turn the clock back
Just for one autumn day,
I would be a little girl
Who dreamed of come-what-may.

Yet, as I watch my little boy
Throw leaves up in the air,
I realize I can't go back
For I am still right there.

When Frost Arrives

Vivian Gilbert Zabel

When frost arrives, it forecasts the end
of sunlight caressing the face and skin,
uplifting the soul with songs of softness.
The fragrance of blooming flowers becomes
the sharpness of fallow, frigid tempests.
Frost frightens away the comfort of Indian Summer,
Leaving a blanket of crimson under maple trees.
Already, blithe breezes of summer have departed,
causing all to snuggle in warm wrappings,
wishing winter had by now come and passed.
A vicious voice whispers through the wind,
bringing threats of a season filled
with blizzards blasting away at life each day.
Yes, when frost arrives, it forecasts
that winter will take the chance of brightness
and substitute the drab, dreary days of adversity.

Inches

Becky L. Simpson

Ever watched an inch worm,
Slowly work its way along,
No clear direction to take.
Worm, does your back ache?
Can you even be that long?
No care to make you squirm.

I want to be an inch worm,
Slow, little, steps as I go
To a goal beyond my sight,
Going from shadow to light,
Getting faster as I grow,
Till on ground standing firm.

Threads

T. Larkin

A stench rises from the swamp,
a malevolent miasma
reminding that life
only grows from death.

Primordial thought lingers here,
single minded pursuit in an endless cycle,
evolved, yet base.

Death feeds life,
and it is not always the strong
that survive the weak,
but a patient eternity
that absorbs all.

Earth, water, rock, and fire are one,
and somewhere in the forest
the full moon watches over a new-born fawn,
and as disassociated as these scenes seem
– swamp and forest –
they are, of course, connected:
Earth, water, rock, and fire,
simple energies feeding each other.

Life itself is a chronometer.
Each body, each entity
contains its own voracious time-line,
feeding from the past to now,
with the future a meal awaiting the tasting.
Yet all are connected,
earth, water, rock, and fire.
Matter cannot be destroyed,
only altered.
Spirit, soul, spark of life,

all must feed on the death of time.

Maybe time is hunger:
the insatiable appetite.
But does the past actually devour the future,
or is the future feeding
on what has come before?

Earth, water, rock, and fire –
spirit, soul, spark of life,
each connected by the tenuous thread of time,
leaving behind nothing by the smell.

Perverse Cat!

Holly Jahangiri

Tiny cat hairs grace my pillow.
I caught her! I'm tempted to laugh.
But one look from Sheba and I
Decide that life's too short as is.

Sunlight bathes her. She licks a paw.
She looks at me as if to say,
"Yeah? What's it to you?" I DON'T laugh.
I do my best to ignore her.

Dignity recovered, Sheba
Pounces on my face, hungrily.
I hasten to make us breakfast.
I like my face the way it is.

Perverse cat. I want to hug her,
But, oh no—she'll have none of that!
It's my bunny slippers she loves.
And my view of Clancy's birdbath.

But sometimes, in the cool evenings,
When there's no one 'round to torture
(Like a mouse) she will warm my lap
And purr, low, as if she means it.

The Sunset

Diane Steele

Motionless and timeless
The sky reflects the hue.
Darkness is upon me --
Orange winks today adieu

The sun has gone adrift
To places I can't see,
Yet I find such peace
As night is now set free.

The sky is specked with light
As each constellation glows.
I look up at the beauty
Which before me simply grows.

I stare across the lake,
A pristine sheet of glass.
I shake my head and smile --
Another day does pass

The sunset brings such peace
For everything feels right.
I thank God for the gift;
Then I say good night.

Mystery

Vivian Gilbert Zabel

Like marshmallow cream piled high in mounds,
miles of clouds, tipped by the sun's golden sheen,
create a carpet of cotton wool,
hiding the world somewhere below.
What could be beneath the snowy blanket?
Do mountains poke and prod,
trying to break through
smothering layers of roiling mist?

Perhaps forests of giant trees
march in endless ranks toward the sky.
A patchwork quilt of living fields
might spread unseen from on high.
Alas, the riders in the red and silver bird
might never know what vistas
they may never see other than
a sky-scape of endless white.

Imperfect Rose

Kimberly Ligameri

I am but a rose,
clothed petals picked-
one by one
nearly
naked to the eye.

My body
stands before you
with each imperfection,
blossomed-
but to you, I am beautiful.

Shadows

Vivian Gilbert Zabel

The shadows from
the towering clouds
create cloaks of shade
across the trees.
The orchard shivers
beneath the sudden chill
as the sun hides its face,
withdrawing its warmth.
Sage warning sound
around the land,
telling all to gather
loved ones near,
to be held close
by arms of love.
Days of laughter, joy
leave much too soon.
People must enjoy
happiness before
it melts under tears
of pounding rain.

Rain Mistress

T. Larkin

I walk through rain as warm as the ages of love -
beginning soft and playful, kissing my cheek,
hesitant and uncertain
before heating up to the coming romance.

With passion now,
scalding in intensity, if not temperature,
the rain embraces me through my clothing,
staking claim to that which is hers.

The darkness of midnight plays with the mood.
I walk from one streetlight to another
as my lover picks up the pace,
with one hand reaching inside my shirt
and another creeping up my thigh.

I open my arms to the sky
allowing myself to be taken.
Moisture runs freely down my face,
indistinguishable from sweat,
as I surrender completely.

She laughs faintly,
thunder in the distance, low and chuckling:
so much a pleased Mistress.
She cups me lovingly,
letting me know she isn't finished.

My Place

Diane Steele

I sat upon the upper deck
and looked up to the sky.
The moon was full, so beautiful.
Translucent clouds sailed by.

The lake spread out, a sheet of glass,
so still and so pristine.
Reflections of the moonlight glow
did complete this perfect scene.

The frogs croaked out a serenade,
as crickets chirped replies.
The lighting for this sweet refrain,
was the darting of fireflies.

My mind was in a special place
which words cannot define.
Existing from, within my heart;
A place that I call mine

I did not stir for quite some time
then left without a care,
knowing that tomorrow night
my place would still be there.

Traces of Autumn

Vivian Gilbert Zabel

Elegantly gowned trees shed their cloaks,
Flooding the ground with a multi-hued quilt
Which weaves a formless pattern,
Smothering the carpet beneath.

Crisp breezes tickle noses
With haunting memories of smoldering leaves
Beneath azure jeweled skies
Teased by veils of misty clouds.

Echoes of cheers, some of jeers,
Escape bleacher-lined fields nearby
Where weary warriors do fight,
Trying a pigskin prize to win.

As chills invade, shivers invoke,
Creating a burning need for fires' flames,
Tiny tots dream of goblins grim
While pumpkins beam gruesome grins.

verbum sap sapienti est
Holly Jahangiri

Barefoot, she runs across the verdant veldt,
rumble-tumble falls down polished, moss-slick
crags and crannies, sparkling translucent jade.
Tumultuous her joy - as overhead
the stately redwoods, timeless cedars fly.

Up, up into the cobalt sky she leaps -
to soar - an eagle o'er the canopy
of lush, exotic, fragrant blooming things.
And at her touch, her kiss, each unripe fruit
attains Spring's first blush and yields its sweetness.

Capricious whims, lightning quick to anger -
verbum sap sapienti est. Thick smoke,
Hell's flames, her ire - yet blackened, charred -
new life still finds a way, as emerald eyes
peek through the cooling ashes of her rage
and blinking up, there sprouts a brand new day.

Misty Mountain Hip-Hop

T. Larkin

It is a grey wool-blanket kind of day;
a mushroom in the cedar
kind of morning – growing clearer
as nearer, ever nearer, seeps the sight
of the new-born sun.
It is a day for everyone to breathe the mist,
to find the morning kissed by dew
amidst the newness
of the few who waited out the night,
only to bloom in the moist breath
of the next day's first-light.

It is a walk down by the river
kind of morning
– kind of shiver –
the Giver has delivered on her promise of the fall.
It is nature's purest call,
a dropping wall of canvas fog
across shoreline, stream, and bog,
over hillside, leaf and log dance lost –
long memory of ancient forest tree
and timeless mountains,
mute — in revere.

Autumn Miracle

Diane Steele

A brilliant hue of color
against the dark, dusk sky,
my eyes do not deceive me
as thunder clouds roll by.

How the beauty can be painted
by Mother Earth's own hand,
I won't begin to ponder
nor try to understand.

Science has a formula
to explain all that I see.
Yet, I hesitate to ask,
just what the cause may be.

The colors of the autumn leaves,
bright yellow, orange, and red,
do leave me with a sense of awe,
explanations best unsaid.

The vision of the colored leaves
silhouette the near-night sky,
bringing memories of autumn dreams,
as years do pass me by.

With every passing year, I see
life in a different light,
yet nothing on this earth can change
the way I feel tonight.

Life's Sunset

Vivian Gilbert Zabel

Dark clouds loom, hiding the horizon.
Thunder-heads build, dimming the sunset,
While overhead the deep blue of a clear sky
Spreads cloudlessly, signaling
A trouble free time of peace.
Yet, fear simmers beneath the calm
As eyes catch a glimpse of the storm's approach.
Joy, laughter leave after a brief visit,
Each seemingly shorter than the last.
Lightning flashes; thunder roars;
Rain beats upon bowed heads
As shoulders heave with sorrow,
The sun banished in the blinding black of night.
Only hope helps keep the heart beating,
Awaiting the next day for cheerful memories.

Winter Blossom

Robert E. Blackwell

There is a singular blossom growing
Through the ivory quilt surrounding it;
Ruby petals glisten with the dew
Of dreams that soak into its dusky cheeks.

The snow-covered ground's slumber continues,
And beneath the surface, gentle heartbeats
Ebb and flow—the Garden's labor pains
Go unnoticed by all save its keeper.

The moon weeps—silvery winter tears
Race to join with their siblings on the quilt;
The blossom stands tall, welcoming the snow
And bidding the Garden sleep until morning.

Wind Dancers

T. Larkin

The wind walks through the forest,
stepping like a dancer
from tree to tree,
touching one here,
bringing it
swaying
into the beat,
skipping past the next two
to favour an Aspen,
playing it
like a milky jade chime.
A singular entity,
the wind circles and moves,
providing music and choreography,
orchestrating
an arboreal ballet.

Love's Lyrics and Laments

Love brings delight and/or despair

Chapter 5
Love's Lyrics and Laments

Song #30

Robert E. Blackwell

Wonder of a heart so pure,
Distant sky of deep azure,
Love set free—the strongest lure,
And I am caught within.

Eyes that sparkle in the sun,
Smile as bright as day begun,
Arms a cradle when day's done
To rest my head therein.

Sharing laughs throughout the day,
Growing close in every way,
Give your ear and let me say
I'm blessed to have you near.

As the moon begins to creep
Through the sky at time to sleep,
Dreams of you are sweet and deep —
My love for you is dear.

You and I

Becky L. Simpson

You and I
Live in love and light,
Love in dignity and grace,
Fulfilling each other's dreams.

We, as one,
Share wealth and poverty,
Give all we have and more,
Sharing each other's dreams.

As family,
We become love's end,
A beginning again,
Teaching our little ones to love.

In the end,
We will find strength
To cross the gulf together,
Our wings touch heaven above.

Closure

Vivian Gilbert Zabel

The young boy's eyes sparkled
As he spied the golden curls
Peeking from under her winter cap.
Since an eight-year-old isn't poetic,
He packed snow into a ball
And threw with all his might,
Knocking the hat from her head.
Imagine his surprise as she whirled
And returned fire, hitting his chest,
Where love for her bloomed.

Over the years, fast friends
They became as they skipped
Hand in hand through school.
His junior prom, she was his date,
As was he for hers the next.
After he left for college,
Letters, like winged flames,
Flew from him to her each week.
The summer became a time of joy
As they rebuilt their love again.

In fall, they had to part once more,
He back to the next level;
She, to the college in town.
Once full of love and laughter,
Messages from her came
Slower and shorter each time.
Soon, by Christmas, they stopped.
By end of semester, he heard
She gave her love to another.
His heart turned to stone.

Years passed, he earned a fortune,
But he never had a family.
At last the loner returned home
To find his lost love not only
Another's wife, but a mother.
He stood in the background,
Knowing her husband could be ruined.

He had the means; he had the hate.
Then he saw her face in his mind
And packed the hate away.

He died the other day:
A driver didn't pause or stop.
Many attended the funeral
With one woman at the back.
Tears pooled and spilled
Before she wiped her face,
Turned, and slipped away.
Only later did she know
He left her not only his heart
But everything he had.

Silences

Robert E. Blackwell

When my words are quiet
And yours are few,
We will speak
In tender glances
With a touch of hands
Joining one to the other.

Kindred hearts know
Every gulf can be spanned
And every gap can be bridged,
Even in silence.

The stillness of our souls
Reflects the depth
Of my serenity in you
And yours in me;
Upon life's river,
We will always sail
Together.

Days of Wine and Roses

Kimberly Ligameri

In the days of wine and roses
We laughed until we cried.
You looked at me
Lovingly, standing by my side.

But just as wine can spoil,
So did your bitter heart.
Now you look at me
Viciously, wishing we were apart.

Like a rose that has withered,
Your love for me has died.
Now you look at me
Unwillingly, pushing me aside.

Song #29

Robert E. Blackwell

Twilight field of starry blossoms shining
Wink in bright patterns that dance in the night;
In love, our hearts and souls intertwining
Nestle in the mellow glow of passion's light.
Kindred spirits, now a constellation,
Live as dreams of a future very bright —
Echoes fill the skies with celebration.

Thunder claps the rhythm of our heartbeats
With lightning dancing counterpoint in sync;
Interludes of love stir passion's drumbeats,
Never shaking the cup from which we drink.
Keys to mind and body we freely share,
Love carries us to Heaven in a blink —
Eternally, we are one with the air.

Memories Of

T. Larkin

Maybe it's reading lines from another life,
perhaps we said it all in Senegal,
and the Roman roads
knew the flavour of our footsteps.

Do you ever dream of remembering me,
of the days when our muses walked with us,

the times of war?

And gently would the words
form and fall,
thick, redolent poetry
sung to the rhythm of clashing swords.

Maybe we were lovers along the Seine...
created memories that never died,
and now the passing of time
knows not what to do with us,

much like
the concept of peace.

The Perfect Poem

Becky L. Simpson

What indeed makes a poem perfect?
Is it form shaped by reflection,
Or perhaps it is pure pleasure?
Maybe the meter is the measure,
That will make the poem perfection.
Oh, to create without defect!

Could be it is no lack of rhyme
Or yet, is it the voiced inflection
That brings us to poetic beauty?
Think you know? Then do your duty:
Tell me what assures selection,
Of words that form a poem sublime.

For I do not know, that is true.
My fate could be to write in prose,
Yet poetry is where my heart beats.
Its beauty my rude skill cheats.
Still one desire in my heart grows:
To pen a perfect poem for you.

Loving Hands

Vivian Gilbert Zabel

Once strong hands now tremble with age,
Still they touch with such tender care
A grandchild handed him to hold,
His wife as she seeks some comfort,
The guitar that he strums in time
To music used, his pain to ease.

Loving hands with aching soreness
Still reach to work, to fix, to mend,
Whether a door, a floor, a heart.
He frets when frustrated, thwarted
In his quest to aid his loved ones,
Because he just no longer can.

Two hands no longer whole, complete
Still show his love through touch, caress.
As he takes others' thrown-away junk,
He fashions objects to be used.
Loving hands need not be spotless
To wipe an errant, helpless tear.

The Village
Robert E. Brackwell

The trees have not become undressed
Around this very sleepy place
Where I first saw, became possessed,
And now am haunted by your face.

The years have quickly passed me by
Since I beheld those calming eyes
That made my anxious spirit fly
To chase the grayness from my skies.

I'd dam the hourglass' sands
To recreate the tender bliss
Of satin skin within my hands,
That held you close for every kiss.

This village town will always hold
The everlasting memory
Of love whose flame since flickered cold
And left me to this reverie.

I'll Never Forget

Kimberly Ligameri

Don't forget the way I smiled
when you kissed my neck.
Don't forget the way my hand
brushed against your chest
everytime we'd lie in bed
waiting for sunrise.
Don't forget how many times
my heart raced
with just the sight of you.
Don't forget the laughter
we shared in our endless nights.

I won't forget how you
were the first to say I love you
underneath the Christmas lights.
I won't forget the roses
you left on my table
for my birthday.
I won't forget our first kiss
when the stars and full moon
shined upon your unforgettable face.
I won't forget our first fight,
or the reconciliation
that lasted for hours.
I won't forget how you broke my heart
when you left me for another.
I won't forget the tears I cried,
praying you'd come running back
into my lonely arms
so I could feel whole again.
I won't forget the day
when you couldn't tell me
that you loved me.
I won't forget the times
when my decisions had to be based
on making your life less complicated,
just so you would love me again.

I won't forget how often you left me
without giving me any reasons.
I won't forget how my heavy heart
felt every time the phone rang

and it wasn't you.

Two Sleepy People (Part II)
Becky L. Simpson

They sit upon the swing talking softly,
Their legs dangling, not quite touching.
Their fingers intertwined like wild roses,
Their faces so close that they touch noses,
Until night is chased by the sun rising.
Still, though tired, their new love burns hotly.

Two sleepy people too much in love to say goodnight.

The next night they sit, once more, in his car.
Snuggled close they can hear each other breathe.
Lips embrace as eyes close for the moment.
Heads angled, they touch in living torment.
They watch the night sky; together they see,
Racing to its destiny, a shooting star.

Two sleepy people too much in love to say goodnight.

Yet another date, they walk matching strides,
Hearts softly beating out music sublime.
They pause; a kiss borne by love is given.
For this they have, against all odds, striven.
He smiles, his eyes bright. Is it ring time?
They walk until in the sky the sun rides.

Two sleepy people too much in love to say goodnight.

Steadfast Heart

Holly Jahangiri

Surely you know what's deep inside –
The words that I too often hide.
Each touch from you, each loving glance –
At once, my heart begins to dance!
Death cannot part us, this I know
For it's my soul that loves you so.
A moment's earthly passion fades;
Still, embers glow among the shades.
Till then, we stand as man and wife;

Hearts joined together, joined for life.
Even anger does not divide;
All arguments are cast aside.
Rare is our love, steadfast and true –
This is my faith – founded on you.

Love Song

Vivian Gilbert Zabel

The man with the rugged face
Gently held her small, soft hand
In his, work-scarred and tough.
His longing look of love
Lanced her heart once more,
Leaving no wound, just joy.
Her smile, still shy, bemused,
Touched his soul again,
As often through their many years.
With her finger, she reached
To stroke his cheek,
Catching an errant tear
He hadn't been able to stop.
Her whispered words,
Barely more than a breath,
Tickled his ear
As he strained to hear.
"Oh, my dear, don't cry.
We won't be parted long.
I'll wait on the other side,
For our love will not die."
He slightly smiled,
Knowing his heart would break.
He knew she was right --
Not even the River Jordan
Could their union divide.

When All the Butterflies Fall

Becky L. Simpson

What do I do when the butterflies fall?
Left feeling so weak and ever so small,
My heart"s desire is just out of reach.
The chasm between us, we tried to breach,
But my love has gone, left me in a mess,
Awash in desires I need to confess.

What do I do when the butterflies fall,
When true love's prince no longer stands tall,
And this new life passes before my eyes?
I can feel it as our short time flies,
My chance for love leaves me behind,
Begging life to slow and for once be kind.

For my love and the sweetness have now left,
Discovering me singing the wrong clef.
I should find again my lost heart and soul,
And seek quiet safe harbor past the shoal.
What do I do when my heart hears its call?
What to do when all the butterflies fall?

Looking at Childhood

Memories, joys, tears, fears, experiences,
dreams of the early years

Chapter 6
Looking at Childhood

Summer Fun

Diane Steele

If I could take my childhood
And pass it on to you,
I'd send you the cottage,
the boat, and lake front, too.

I will never have the means
To purchase all I had,
Turning precious memories
To thoughts that make me sad.

Yet, my son, I know you well --
The cottage, never known,
Is replaced by happiness
We find all on our own.

You spend the lazy, hazy days
Finding simple pleasure
In the memories we create,
Forever yours to treasure.

For the simple things in life
Are those we can afford.
The bond between us tightens,
Shared love our sweet reward.

Just Wanna Pout!

Holly Jahangiri

I won't be nice, don't wanna play!
I'm feeling out of sorts today.
I hate my room, I hate my toys -
Just wanna shout and make some noise!

Today I'm feeling out of sorts,
Don't like baseball - don't like SPORTS!
I wanna scream, I wanna shout,
I wanna fuss, I wanna pout.

Don't like sports - no, not at all.
Don't throw me that old basketball!
I only wanna pout and whine;
I won't be nice. No, I'm NOT fine.

Hey, that basketball looks kinda fun.
Could we - maybe? One on one?
I'm in a better mood, of course -
Now how 'bout we play some HORSE?

Rain Dancer

Kimberly Ligamerii

She moves like rain
in melodies and styles,
washing away her pain
pirouetting across the miles.

Sun gleams
upon her face,
as her dance dreams
of beauty and grace.

Tiny rain-dancing feet
tiptoe and glide,
so precious, so sweet
right by my side.

Smudges

Vivian Gilbert Zabel

Tiny fingerprint smudges,
On the windows of memory,
Leave reminders that tickle my mind
As once again I see baby faces
Pressed against the glass, looking back at me.
From the past to the present, time passes.
The children have grown until adults exist.
No longer chubby, faces beam with smiles,
Unless I tightly squint,
Then briefly find remnants
Of the cherubs they used to be.
The dimple once deep in a cheek
Now slightly hints
When the one son grins.
The younger now covers the cleft
In his chin with a man's beard.
The woman's blue eyes still twinkle
With mischief hidden within.
Shadow smudges remain dimly real.

Where Did the Time Go?
Diane Steele

My son was whining endlessly-
I thought I'd lose my mind.
I wanted but one moment
to sit and just unwind.

My patience was so very short;
Work had caused some strife.
I gazed into the living room
and realized my whole life

sat sadly on the sofa,
toys scattered all around.
I watched him for a moment,
trying not to make a sound.

I then sat down beside him;
we talked about his day.
His voice so very cheerful,
he had so much to say

The thoughts that he conveyed
Made one thing very clear:
(A sadness overwhelmed me,
bringing to my eye, a tear.)

He had lived a lifetime,
Now so suddenly mature.
Thoughts of missing one more day,
my heart could not endure.

It took such little effort
To sit beside my boy.
He really didn't need
the TV or a toy.

Is Cleanliness Next to Godliness?

Holly Jahangirii

They say that cleanliness is loved by God,
And so I clean, with duty as my guide,
and obligation. Yet, when I behold
these sparkling baseboards - have I sinned in pride?

Debased (and bored) I scrub and scrub and scrub,
Martyr to my ceramic-tiled hall
On which my children run with sullied feet
While leaving grubby hand prints on the wall.

I pray I go to heaven long before
My children come a-knocking on God's door.
A brief respite, that's all I ask of Him:
Self-cleaning carpet and self-mopping floor.

Surely I won't cry out in prideful sin--
"They're filthy, God! How can you let them in?"

A Day in the Park
(A Poem in Virelay Form)
Vivian Gilbert Zabel

Boys and girls, all awhirl, swing and laugh having fun.
Children scamper and fall,
As across the playground parents sit on benches in the
sun,
Most glad they aren't inside at the mall.

A group of older youth gather for a game of baseball
With friends ready to cheer
For each team's score or against the umpire's call,
At times, for which unclear.

A time and place of fellowship for all without fear
Beneath the shading trees,
Everyone can and does enjoy the pleasures here,
Even the buzzing of the bees.

For each, here and now, can enjoy the bright, warm
breeze,
The peaceful lull.
Too soon comes chilling winds that pave the leas*
For winter's cold pall**

•   *leas means pastures*
*** pall means gloom or cloud-covered*

Forget-Me-Not

Diane Steele

My son came bounding through the door,
as happy as could be.
A bouquet of Forget-Me-Nots
was what he had for me.

I thought about that simple act
and had no time to say
exactly how I felt, for he
rushed back out to play.

My son had thought, if only for
one moment of his day,
of sending just a little piece
of heartfelt love my way.

I really do so need the flowers
my son did give to me.
A reminder of how blessed I am,
I look at them and see

all that I am thankful for
today and everyday,
Knowing more Forget-Me-Nots
again will come my way.

The Slugger

Robert E. Blackwell

The slugger digs in at the plate,
His eyes transfixed upon his prey;
Determination in his brow,
Anticipation rules the day.

The moments pass before he sees
A globe of white has taken flight —
Its rate of speed a daunting thing,
And yet, it stays within his sight.

With lightning streaking toward the plate,
His thunder steady in his hands,
He swings......and with a mighty "CRACK!"
The ball departs for distant lands.

He runs the bases, jubilant
As friends and neighbors shout his name;
The slugger shares his joy with all
Who came to see his first ball game.

A Purple Gift

Diane Steele

I picked a purple flower
from the field beside my house.
I tip-toed to the kitchen,
    as quiet as a mouse.

I climbed onto the counter,
which I'm not supposed to do.
I knew it was okay this once,
and soon my mom would, too.

I found the vase I knew was there
and slid back to the floor.
Then I scooted across the room
and right back out the door.

The hose looked like a giant snake
curled upon the grass.
I picked it up and placed it so
the last few drops did pass

    into the vase so slowly,
    yet just enough you see,
    that it was not quite full,
        nor was it empty.

I smiled and so gently
placed my flower there,
then bounced back to kitchen
without a single care.

I looked into the living room
and saw Mom drinking tea.
I held out my purple present.
She was as happy as could be.

She held me tight and whispered
right into my ear,
"Thank you very much, my love."
I heard it loud and clear.

Dylan

Kimberly Ligameri

My blue-eyed son,
at night I sit
watching you breathe.
As you sleep,
your precious legs
curl and cross,
and your tiny hands close-
as if they were
holding mine.
As you dream of
sunshine, rainbows, and stars,
I find your
sweet smiling lips.
Leaning closer I whisper,
"I love you from the moon and back,"
in those darling ears.
With the scent of lavender and honey
lingering through the room,
I remember
the years will fly by,
and someday you will leave,
but
my dear blue-eyed son
I will still be
watching you breathe.

A Hat Full of Sky

Diane Steele

I have a very special cap,
As special as can be.
I wear it everywhere I go
for all the world to see.

My mom says, "Take that cap off,"
when I sit down at the table.
I quickly put it on again
as soon as I am able.

At night when I am sleeping,
It sits beside my bed.
When I awake, it's waiting
to sit upon my head.

My baseball cap is red and white.
I'm very proud of it.
When I put it on my head,
it's a perfect fit.

The visor is always there
to keep the sun out of my eyes.
I can catch most anything,
from grounders to pop flies.

And when another game is won,
I bet you can guess why
I throw my cap with all my might
way up towards the sky.

Dancing Dragon

Holly Jahangirii

When I awoke this morning,
at the first cold light of dawn,
I looked outside and found
A dancing dragon on the lawn.

He did a soft-shoe shuffle;
Then he doffed his hat, you see.
"I'll believe in you," he said,
"If you'll believe in me."

Well, little did the dragon know
That I was predisposed
To trust in anything with wings.
But now I'm sure he knows.

A dragon's laughter brightly burns
And cauterizes pain.
For when a dancing dragon laughs,
Dark thoughts cannot remain.

The neighbors think I've lost my mind.
Perhaps I have, at that.
My mother wonders why
I'm not content with just a cat.

They say they wouldn't let
A dragon on their lawns to graze.
They fear he'll set the house afire
Amidst the games he plays.

Well, if the house goes up in flames,
There'll be a weenie roast.
We'll warm ourselves before the blaze
And drink a friendly toast.

Fine houses are on every street,
But dancing dragons, well...
When you'll find another's something
You can never tell.

I wouldn't chain him if I could,
He'll wander where he will.
But I can hope when next I look
He's dancing out there, still.

Despair

Vivian Gilbert Zabel

Child-woman, lost, lonely,
Broken heart hidden
Within a storm of pain,
Stands buffeted by wounding winds
Beyond her waning strength.

Around her bowed head,
Flowing locks swirl,
Blinding eyes dimmed by dying tears.
Longing for peace, for comforting arms
Not provided by those who should,
Becomes a bludgeoning burden
Forcing slender shoulders
Ever lower to the ground.

Caused too young to carry weight
Of those much older,
Torn between conflicting loyalties,
She collapses, knees skinned,
Emotions battered, bruised,
Becoming another of life's casualties,
Her desire drowning in despair.

How Do Reindeer Fly?
Diane Steele

"Mom, can reindeer really fly?
If they can, then tell me why
they only fly one night a year;
and why it is I never hear

them come and go on Christmas Eve?
How do you expect me to believe?
We have no chimney, that you know.
How does Santa come and go?"

"My precious child, sit down with me,
and I will try to help you see
the way it happens Christmas Eve.
Now close your eyes and just believe.

"No one knows the reason why
reindeer sail into the sky,
or how they land on top of roofs
without us hearing pounding hoofs.

"How does Santa find his way
to our tree by Christmas Day?
Twas a magical, wondrous, mystery
when Rudolph did make history."

"So you need not wonder why,
for no matter how you try,
only Santa knows the way
to bring you joy on Christmas Day.

"Remember son, one special thought:
The birth of Jesus to us brought
all the things you hold so dear
today and everyday each year."

The Faces on Milk Cartons

Kimberly Ligameri

They weren't just faces
Painted on milk cartons.
They were alive;
They were free.
They loved life.
They were somebody's children.
How could someone be so heartless?
It is by God's hands they were born,
And only His hands should take them.

I saw her skipping down the street
Barefoot and pigtailed,
Laughing with the sun.
Her sapphire eyes sparkled
With innocence and love.
With her laughter echoing
In my thoughts,
I am reminded,
She was alive.
She was free.
She loved life.
She was someone's child.
She is a memory,
A memory I hold dear.

How could someone be so heartless?
It is by God's hands they were born,
And only His hands should take them.
They weren't just faces
painted on milk cartons.
They were alive;
They were free.
They loved life.
They were somebody's children.

My Best Friend

Robert E. Blackwell

Back in the day,
My best friend was a shiny gold bike
With five speeds and a banana seat.
She was powered by the twin pistons
Of matchstick legs pumping endless
Twinkie-filled energy.
Anyone else saw a child's bike,
But she was anything I thought of
And everything I'd dreamed about.
She was my private roller coaster
Down the steep, narrow paths
Of Clifton Park's apartments.
Past the schoolyard grounds,
I was "all that," cruising by
In my sleek, slick Cadillac.
The alleys were uncharted worlds,
Waiting for me and my rocket ship
To explore their mysterious passages.

Above all else,
She was my friend
When no one else would be.

Who needed to conquer the world
When my bike and I had one
Of our very own?

Growing Older

The memories, fears, tears, dreams,
experiences of aging

Chapter 7
Growing Older

Lost Memory
Vivian Gilbert Zabel

Memories tease with a tempting taste of yesterday
Then flicker away before I can fully favor the flavor,
Leaving a vague sense in the back of my brain
Of something no longer there, of something gone.
I search in dark, dank corners, hidden places,
Brushing strands of spider webs away as they cling,
Tangling me in sticky gossamer nets and snares.
Finally, I spy a tattered ancient trunk under piles
Of pitiful, plentiful mounds of dirt and dust mites.
I silently slip to lift the lid, seeking a secret desire,
Wanting to find at last what I no longer have:
My wandering, rambling, forgotten, lost mind.

Recollections of an Old Man

Kimberly Ligameri

Sitting in an overstuffed chair
with saddened eyes and whitened hair,
thinking about journeys in life,
remembering his lovely wife,
he longed to hold her slender hand
that once wore a gold wedding band.
Feeling like a crumbling rock,
carrying too much pain to block,
swollen lumps in his throat remain,
teardrops pouring down like blue rain.
Light from a lamp begins to fade
as he continuously prayed
for God to bless his aching heart,
for his life once again to start.

Music of Goodbye

T. Larkin

Play me out the door,
a slow blues number with a gentle hook,
something with a walking bass so I can practice my
strut,
and a piano.
There has to be a piano.

Play me solid music
with bones that rattle to shake the dust,
something that cleans the sky, sweeping the clouds
away
as my shoes
would clear the sidewalk.

Play me down the road
with a tune that implies light in the dark,
something where the singer recalls the stars in the
night,
while an echo
recalls the passing of my feet.

Play me goodbye
on an old, abused record player,
something with a blunt needle and a quarter on the
arm,
and let the notes
fade away along with me.

If I Had

Diane Steele

If I had a penny,
I know I'd want a dime.
If I had a million,
All I'd want is time.

Life's too short to gamble;
I always would want more,
Forgetting all the triumphs
That I had made before.

No value can be placed
On happiness or treasures,
Those memories kept stored away
As our lives' simple pleasures.

Time cannot be measured
By materialistic things,
Yet I feel so rich inside
As each new daybreak brings

A time to spend with family,
A son whom I adore
Memories that make me smile --
These and so much more.

When I go to bed each night,
I thank Him for the time.
I know that I have billions,
A penny, and a dime.

Some Day

Vivian Gilbert Zabel

Some day, my love,
we'll stand hand in hand,
no pain nor worry
to tie us to this land.
We shall run nimbly
as children do,
jumping, skipping
across seas of cloud.
The toils and trials
we face each day
will not be ours,
but will be packed away.
Then you can again
look at me
through eyes young
enough to clearly see.
I'll touch your face
with fingers
no longer gnarled
or twisted with age.
Some day, our treasure
of teeming joy
shall not be
tempered or spoiled
with earthly
trouble or despair.
Memory will not
any longer matter,
for our minds
shall be as new.
Some day, ah, yes,
a thought even better,
we will never
have to say adieu.

Memories from a Dresser Drawer
Kimberly Ligameri

In my dresser drawer
I stumbled across your picture,
faded and scratched
like our relationship became.
I tried to throw it away but
found myself staring into your eyes,
wanting you to come back home.

In my dresser drawer
I found your old letters,
crumpled and torn
like our relationship became.
I should have discarded them, but
instead I was drawn back to your love,
dreaming you were in my life again.

Outside the store window
I saw you today,
kissing someone
like you used to kiss me.
I needed to ignore what I saw, but,
of course, I cried,
wishing I could be that someone.

Time Passes

Vivian Gilbert Zabel

Once his touch ignited feelings
She didn't know existed.
She surrendered to his loving care
When young, naive, virtuous.
Hand in hand they became one.
Time passes.

Once busy with life, with children,
No space or minutes to call theirs,
His touch brought embers back
To flame when least expected,
Stolen moments belonging to them.
Time passes.

Now they alone fill their home.
Rooms empty, numbers of hours
Surround them in a timeless embrace.
At his trembling touch, her eyes drift close,
Their love enclosing them once more.
Time passes until gone.

Dedicated to my husband, Robert

Growing Old

Diane Steele

Your image always there to see,
Framed memories on the wall,
I gaze up at your timeless face
Just so I can recall

The carefree days when we were young.
Time forever on our side,
We danced into the golden years;
With each heartbeat, we did glide,

Those days were ours to have and hold,
Yet our grasp was growing weak.
Grey hair and wrinkles, the silent truths
Of those, we did not speak.

Agelessness, we knew, was just a dream,
And still we did not fear.
Although your time did come, my love,
Memories grow with each New Year.

My world is not the same, it's true,
Yet life has been so kind.
For with each new passing year
More memories fill my mind.

The Next Station

Robert E. Blackwell

Somewhere in the far beyond,
When we pay the tab for this life
And take the shuttle to the next,
If we're both on the same train,
I'll let you sit by the window
If you let me rest my head
On your shoulder
And wake me when we get there.

Promise me that whoever
Gets to the next station first
Will wait for the other to arrive;
If it's me I'll wear only a flower
With a single dream blossom on the stem.

If you get there before I do,
Turn on the music of the honeybee
(Whose buzzing reminds me of a lullaby
Sung by a new mother at dusk)
And save every dance for me.

River of Life

Vivian Gilbert Zabel

Beside the woman, the river flows
Bringing images to her mind.

Lo, leaning against a tree
Stands her daughter,
Her long hair blowing free,
Yet, not her daughter,
Her granddaughter there instead.

In the woman's arms lies her son,
But, no, 'tis his son she holds,
Laughing, gurgling baby talk.
Only memories of what had been
His eyes, his tiny hands do mock.

Beside the woman in a bed,
The river shows a man with silver in his hair.
Lines and creases years have pressed
Upon his once young face
Where now care and pain do rest.

The current flowing ever on
Mirrors the reflection of her mother's face
On the water's glassy dull glare.
Unbelieving, the woman looks again,
But all that returns is her mother's stare.

In the river, as the woman gazes,
Close the pages of her life's book.

Life is a Lesson

Diane Steele

So many hurdles I did jump
To still be here today.
I'd rather look at rainbows
Than look the other way.

I think there is a treasure
In everybody's life.
Our vision has to look beyond
The things that cause us strife.

I have had my share of bad,
Now searching for the light,
My eyes still fixed upon the gold
That casts a shine so bright.

I can go ahead in life,
Strive for so much more
Knowing I can only change
Mistakes I made before.

Should I not complete this task,
I will still feel fine
In knowing I did try my best
To achieve all that is mine.

Our Years

Becky L. Simpson

Over the years,
Through the tears,
You have been by my side.
Walking along the shore,
You kept back life's rude tide,
Asking me to be your
True love.

You have been
My hands, pen,
And sparkle in the sand
Falling through the hourglass.
Beside me do you stand.
Arm in arm do we pass,
Our time.

Now we grow,
Oh, so slow,
Following a silver moon,
Racing the bright sunrise.
Knowing that all too soon,
Love in us will surprise
Our souls.

Woman in the Glass
Vivian Gilbert Zabel

Who is that woman in the glass with care-worn face
And a relentless sorrow deep within her gaze?
Her hair, once dark now faded, hides threads of white.
Lines of laughter and of pain feather across planes no
longer young.
Who is that woman in the glass
Whose lips tip upward in a smile as if hearing some
hidden jest,
Yet at times move in silent prayer or droop in
discouragement?
How familiar she appears,
This aged woman whose tiredness shimmers through
the reflected image.
Apparently she hears not the youth, the life, the joy
singing from my heart.
Who is that woman in the glass?
Could this my mother be,
her great-grandson at her breast?
Ah, no, I can't believe what I see.
That haggard old woman is actually me.

Traveling in Faith

Walking in the light, praying, testing, living, failing, succeeding.

Chapter 7
Traveling in Faith

Have I Sinned in Pride? (A Prayer)

Holly Jahangiri

It is said you never heap upon us
More sorrows and trials than we can bear;
Sometimes you give me too much credit, God -
Or is it that you're distant, you don't care?

Or is it that you're near to me, and I
Have sinned - unknowing - arrogant with pride -
Believing I could stand the heavy load
Without complaint or aid? Oh, God...I've cried.

And yet, I haven't crumpled, begged for help;
I haven't yet been forced on bended knee.
Through joy and grief alike, I have stood tall

And asked for nothing. Now I say, *Hear ME.*

For others whom I love, in need, I pray -
And God? The load's enough, for now...today.

Think of Good Things

Robert E. Blackwell

Philippians 4:8

Think of the things that make you glad:
Thoughts that bring laughter when you're sad,
Favorite things you like to do,
Songs you can sing when feeling blue.

Chase away thoughts that make you mad;
Don't believe those who say you're bad.
Always keep rainbows in your mind,
Thinking of all things good and kind.

The Light that Shines

Jacque Graham

My God is the light
That must shine through my love.
He is the ultimate source.
The light of my life is lasting and true:
A gift of God's own true "love-force."

He pours out His light
On each of us now
Through His own true Spirit divine.
He labels us for the world to see.
"This precious child is mine."

Our lamp is lighted
With God's love flame
So we can be set on the hill.
And the world can see that He is the light
And that He gives His guidance still.

His word is a light
On our darkest paths
And a lamp to our stumbling feet.
As we walk through life lifting high His flame
To each stranger and friend that we meet.

God lit His lamps
For a purpose - a task.
A special mission is ours.
We must carry the light to the darkest domains,
The valleys, and high-rising towers.

On the pathways we take
O'er life's winding roads,
Through valleys and by rocky rills,
We lift His flame high for a light to our feet

And let His light shine as He wills.

To let our light shine before men
Is our task,
That glory may be to the Father.
As our light glows with God's love
We may light the path for another.

This is the task
For which we are called.
His Love is the light we lift high,
That others may feel the warmth of the flame
And see our God walking by.

The light of our soul
Is a flickering flame.
Its glow is soft - sometimes dim -
Until the flame is fed with His Love,
And it shines more brightly with Him.

Our flame is but one,
Fed by faith and by hope.
It alone cannot light the whole earth.
But each one who comes to the Savior anew
Lights a corner with the flame of rebirth.

Each soul who lights the candle of Love
And reaches out to another
Lets His light so shine,
And the flame is spread
From child to sister to brother.

Our light must spread
O'er all the earth
Into darkest corners and bright,
That God's great love might enfold the earth
And chase away Sin's fearful night.

"I am the Light of the World,"
My heavenly Father declared.
I could give light to another,
Only in faith,
As I dared,

Giving of myself to another
Or to a child as he cried.
'Twas to give me this power,
To love the unlovely,
That my Savior was beaten and died.

But even in death,
His light was bright.
His love was not crucified.
Only in the power of His love
Will life remain, though we've died.

Yes, this is the task
For which we are called.
His Love is the Light we lift high.
That others may feel the warmth of the flame
And see our God walking by.

The Gardener

Robert E. Blackwell

Behold the Gardener's children:
Colorful flowers lovingly planted,
Watered with tears of love
And warmed by the sun of caring.

Each tender reed is encouraged
To grow strong and blossom freely,
Nourishing the world
With the wisdom of its petals.

Each flower is known by its name
And the scent of its nature,
Just as each flower knows its nurturer
And the endless love given it.

The world turns outside the Garden,
And the flowers bear witness to all times,
Yet remain untroubled by them;
They flourish and thrive in the Gardener's care.

May it ever be so.

Forever Love

Vivian Gilbert Zabel

A child lies crying silently in the night.
She heard her parents have another fight.
Through her mind echoes her father's words,
"Nothing lasts forever. I don't love you anymore."

A man lies in the gutter cursing loudly,
While a cry for help he issues quietly.
His life in shambles is all he sees,
No reason left to live, nothing remains but pain.

A woman falls on her knees in bitter shame.
No one else, just herself can she blame.
Her own selfishness led to her ruin,
Leaving her but one final name for help to pray.

An old man sits rocking, staring at the wall.
Months go by, and his children never call.
He feels forgotten and all alone
As his life slips by in a blind and mindless fog.

But love forever can be found
In the name of Jesus,
Love forever for all who need
A never dying, forever living,
Forever lasting love.

My Lighthouse

Kimberly Ligameri

I once walked in doubt and shame,
carrying only vanity and pride.
Then along You came,
My Lord, my Lighthouse, my Guide.

I once was drowning in uncertainty and greed,
losing myself in tears I have cried.
Then You planted the seed,
My Lord, my Lighthouse, my Guide.

I once possessed feelings of hatred and despair,
living without You by my side.
Then because of You, my life was spared,
My Lord, my Lighthouse, my Guide.

I once was full of jealousy and dismay,
refusing to turn and confide.
Then I saw the truth, the life, the way,
My Lord, my Lighthouse, my Guide.

Jesus Wept

Becky L. Simpson

John 11:35

Jesus Wept

My favorite verse,
No words more powerful
Can lips' width transverse
Nor comfort bring pain's lull.

He loves us, His sheep.
Our loss His heart knew.
He for our death did weep.
Did we give His its due?

Yes, short it may be,
Yet clear is its cause.
I know He loves me,
Despite all my flaws,

Jesus wept.

Upon My Death

Jacque Graham

He kept me day by day
In this earthly walk;
Now, friend to friend,
Our spirits talk.

All earthly needs
He provided here,
Much greater His provision
As death draws near.

I walked the earth with Him.
I passed the great test.
In death, at His bosom
I find comfort and rest.

Upon my death I pray
All will rejoice.
I would tell you,
Could I, with human voice,

"Now
With my Father
I shall dwell.
All things are well!"

Blinded

Vivian Gilbert Zabel

My eyes, so often blind,
At times refuse to see
God's mighty hand
Reaching down for me.
Absorbed in my own way,
I lack insight to know
His plan is wise,
If my will I let go.
Then when feeling lost, alone,
I ask where God has gone.
His voice, soft and close,
Suggests my eyes open wide
To find He has been by my side -
All the time.

Of Angels' Wings

Becky L. Simpson

A baby born is borne
In the bosom of angels' wings.
A soul is brought home torn and worn
by a flight of angels' wings

A love began so strong is carried into the air
By the beating heart of angels' wings.
My life, my love, if I only dare,
Soars to heights unknown on angels' wings.

In failure, the warmth of knowing love
Resides in the folds of angels' wings.
One day I shall see that love flowing
As God gives me my own set of angel's wings.

Conversation with God

Kimberly Ligameri

Father, I have a heavy heart
filled with sorrow and woe.
I haven't an idea where to start,
but my salted tears must flow.
You look to me with gentle eyes
and tenderly take my hand
whispering, "Child, you must realize
things don't always go as planned."

Father, I have a troubled mind
cluttered with confusion and fear.
I am losing faith in mankind
with every passing year.
You hold me very close,
aware of my sadness and pain,
whispering, "Child, don't lose faith in those
who are living their lives in vain."

Father, I have a lonely soul
consumed by empty feeling.
I am restless and cold,
and my layers are slowly peeling.
You console me by erasing my concern,
protecting me from this world's mass,
whispering, "Child, though your life may turn,
always remember, and this too shall pass."

Pastel Memories

Diane Steele

Pastel colored memories
of Easters I did know,
patent leather upon my feet
did catch the sun's bright glow.

Young and so carefree the days
of innocent, youthful bliss,
lilacs perfumed petals,
each held a dew drop's kiss.

Chocolate covered treasures,
the kind that do not last,
for as I grew older,
reality scarred the past.

Church bells rang a sweet refrain
to welcome from the dead
one who gave His life, and, yet,
more lives still lost instead.

Pastel colors faded fast.
My shoes no longer shined,
carefree days long gone now.
The world, somehow, turned blind.

As church bells chimed a sweet refrain,
bombs exploded in their wake.
Rejoice for He has risen!
And, yet, I could not take

My eyes off of His portrait,
where He hung nailed upon a cross,
To die for us and rise to see
a world so full of loss.

The Choice

Vivian Gilbert Zabel

When the future darkly looms,
Not one light to mark the way,
Prayer provides the power,
Our permission for His return.

When by the world sight is screened,
Hidden is His presence's light.
Darkness shrouds life's narrow path
While souls die in the blinding murk.

Judgment brings eternal doom
To those who refuse to see,
Heeding not the Lord's strong call
To return to His loving fold.

Prayer, asking forgiveness,
Will divide the gloom in two,
Permitting love to brighten
The path from which man mustn't swerve.

Yet, He leaves the choice to man
Whether the future will be
In Heaven spent forever
Or eternity spent in Hell.

Forgive Me, Father

Kimberly Ligameri

If I have turned my back on those in need,
if I have been hateful toward another,
if I have been selfish and full of greed,
if I could have been a better mother,
Father, I pray that You forgive me,
and I know that You will.
You will hear my plea
and love me still.

If I have uttered something I regret,
if I have wandered and fell off track,
if I have gossiped about someone I met,
if I have been shoved and I pushed back,
Father, I pray that You forgive me,
and I know that You will.
You will hear my plea
and love me still.

If I have worried about a frivolous task,
if I have not always had the right thing to say,
if I have taken before I ask,
if I have been ungrateful in any way,
Father, I pray that You forgive me,
and I know that You will.
You will hear my plea
and love me still.

If I have an indecent thought,
if I could have helped more,
if I have overlooked something I should have taught,
if I have ever felt angry or sore,
Father, I pray that you forgive me,
and I know that You will.
You will hear my plea

and love me still.

Father, I know that you hear my prayer,
and You will not abandon or ignore.
I know that You are never unfair.
You will be waiting for me upon Your shore
with open arms forgiving my mistakes,
letting me start a life fresh and new,
erasing the pain of this world's aches.
You will take me into Heaven and I'll reside with You.

Heaven Waits

Vivian Gilbert Zabel

Heaven can wait and does,
Silently, patiently just past
Human sight and notice.
Yes, heaven may wait, but can I?
My body aches, wracked with pain,
My mind with cares and fears.
Peace cannot be found in a heart
Breaking with loss, disappointments.
Dreams dashed beyond repair,
Hopes never realized
Bring longing for that mansion
Promised in God's book.
A whisper barely heard
Tickles my ear;
I am not alone,
My burden mine to bear.
He walks beside me
Guiding, leading all the way.
Then, when He decides I need not wait,
He will show me heaven's gate.

Hilltops

Jacque Graham

Tonight I stood on a hilltop;
I know not why.
The wind blew, hit me,
Then passed me by.
I ran down,
Down, through flowers dense.
I was free and lacked all sense
Of time as I ran on.
I came to a wood.
The trees stood tall,
And still I ran on,
Unthinking through all.
I stumbled and fell,
And opening my eyes,
I beheld a small cloud
Pasted on reverent skies.
I lay in a trance
For the longest while....
Then I knew.

Tonight I stood on a hilltop;
I know now why.
God led me there
In the windy still.
He led me there
To show His will.
Then I see and run
And exhausted fall,
And He'll pick me up
When I answer His call.

Everybody Everywhere
Becky L. Simpson

Everybody everywhere,
No matter what one's station,
Has moments of deep loneliness
And quiet desperation,
For this lost and lonely feeling
Is inherent in mankind –

It is just the Spirit speaking,
As God tries again to find
An opening in the "worldly wall"
Man builds against God's touch,
For man feels so self sufficient
That he does not need God much.
Hence he vainly goes on struggling
To find some explanation
For these disturbing lonely moods
Of inner isolation.

But the answer keeps eluding him,
For in his selfish finite mind,
He does not even recognize
That he cannot ever find
The reason for life's emptiness
Unless he learns to share
The problems and the burdens
That surround him everywhere –

But when his eyes are opened
And he looks with love at others,
He begins to see not strangers
But understanding brothers.
So open up your hardened hearts.
And let God enter in –

He only wants to help you
A new life to begin,
And every day's a good day
To lose yourself in others.
Anytime is a good time
To see mankind as brothers,
And this can only happen
When you realize it's true
That everyone needs someone -
That someone is you.

A Gentle Touch

Vivian Gilbert Zabel

A gentle touch
    of a mother's loving palm
    upon a fevered brow,
A gentle touch
    of a baby's small hand
    upon his father's face,

A gentle touch
    of conscience's pull
    upon a guilty mind
Is nothing compared to
    the gentle touch
        of the Spirit's call
        upon a sinner's soul,

A gentle touch
    of perfect love
    upon the troubled heart,
The gentle touch
    of Jesus' love
    upon the hate-filled world.

War at Easter Time

Diane Steele

Lucky are those who will wake up tomorrow
sheltered from poverty, hunger and sorrow.
Sheltered from violence, Easter treats do abound
while the rest of our world is turned upside down.

Lucky are those whose loved ones are near
with them at Easter, with nothing to fear.
Yet, those at war do bear a great cross,
feeling the pain of sorrow and loss.

Lucky are those who will find but a crumb
to lessen the hunger to which they succumb,
while missiles continue to fly overhead,
knowing loved ones are presumably dead.

Courageous are those who strive to help out.
They will be remembered without any doubt.
The love and commitment they offer is clear,
bringing us hope as Easter draws near.

His Church

Jacque Graham

On the byways,
Near the highways,
Stands a structure
Strong and sure.

And the steeple
And its people
Preach of Love
So sweet and pure.

Christ came to Earth
Of human birth
So God could
Draw us near.

He shared God's love,
Brought from above
The end of
All our fear.

His church stands strong
Against the wrongs
Of yesteryear
And now.

If we would hear
The truths so dear,
Our lives would change
I vow.

Appendix A
Biographies

Robert E. Blackwell hails from Columbus, Ohio, where he lives with his family. He has work published in a number of anthologies. Published collections include *The Ten-Digit Poet* (August, 2004) and *Sunshine for the Soul* (April, 2005).

A native of a small town in Oklahoma and the grandmother of six, **Jacque Graham** taught English and composition for thirty years. She writes mainly poetry and has for most of her life. Her work has been published in magazines and anthologies. Much of her poetry revolves around her faith and her family.

Holly Jahangiri is a professional writer with over twenty years' experience in technical writing, freelancing, and editing. On a good writing day, she claims (tongue-in-cheek) to be channeling the spirits of Edgar Allan Poe, Erma Bombeck, and O. Henry. On a bad writing day, she claims to have poured every last ounce of her creative ability and energy into childbirth. She has two wonderful children – her son, William, and her daughter, Katie – to prove it. But regardless of whether it's a good day or a bad day, she is grateful for the love and support of J.J., her husband of twenty years

Tim Larkin is a west coast Canadian living outside of Vancouver. He says that growing up between mountains and ocean helped to shape his writing, giving him a love of nature while showing him the scope of grandeur. Tim has made his living in many various ways, from door-to-door sales to operating a metal spinning lathe, and currently works in a glass factory building patio doors. Tim discovered his writing talent late in life and has only been at it for the last few years, but says he looks forward to seeing where it leads him.

Kimberly Ligameri began writing poetry when she was sixteen. She used writing as a tool to express and release emotions and ideas. In the past two years, she had her poetry published in two books, *Garden of Gems* and *Expressions on Matters of Faith and Reverence*. Kimberly looks forward to future opportunities.

A native Floridian, **Becky Simpson** moved to Tennessee to pursue a career in Electrical Engineering. She recently took up writing as a way of expressing her life experiences. Poetry, her preferred medium, helps her avoid the pitfalls of blondeness; with poetry's concise structure she can't get lost.

Diane Steele is an Early Childhood Educator who loves to read and write in her spare time. Her dream is to improve her writing and publish a book for children. With an 8-yr-old son and full time job, this may be a long time coming. She has escaped the here-and-now through poetry. Her poems are simplistic, from the heart and always inspired by the events of daily life.

A retired teacher, **Vivian Gilbert Zabel** has written and studied poetry since she was in the third grade. She says she thinks in poetry and has to translate into prose. Her work centers around life experiences (including life in Oklahoma) and her family: her husband Robert, who is her strongest supporter, her children, grandchildren, and great-grandchildren. Her poetry has appeared in anthologies and magazines. One book of her poetry, *Reflected Images*, is now out of print.

Index